ABOUT THE BANK STREET READY-TO-READ SERIES

Seventy years of educational research and innovative teaching have given the Bank Street College of Education the reputation as America's most trusted name in early childhood education.

Because no two children are exactly alike in their development, we have designed the *Bank Street Ready-to-Read* series in three levels to accommodate the individual stages of reading readiness of children ages four through eight.

- *Level 1:* GETTING READY TO READ—read-alouds for children who are taking their first steps toward reading.
- *Level 2:* READING TOGETHER—for children who are just beginning to read by themselves but may need a little help.
- ○ *Level 3:* I CAN READ IT MYSELF—for children who can read independently.

Our three levels make it easy to select the books most appropriate for a child's development and enable him or her to grow with the series step by step. The *Bank Street Ready-to-Read* books also overlap and reinforce each other, further encouraging the reading process.

We feel that making reading fun and enjoyable is the single most important thing that you can do to help children become good readers. And we hope you'll be a part of Bank Street's long tradition of learning through sharing.

The Bank Street
College of Education

THE COLOR WIZARD
A Bantam Little Rooster Book
Simultaneous paper-over-board and trade paper editions/July 1989

Little Rooster is a trademark of Bantam Books,
a division of Bantam Doubleday Dell Publishing Group, Inc.

Series graphic design by Alex Jay/Studio J
Associate Editor: Randall Reich

Special thanks to James A. Levine, Betsy Gould, and
Erin B. Gathrid.

Library of Congress Cataloging-in-Publication Data
Brenner, Barbara.
The color wizard.

(Bank Street ready-to-read)
''A Byron Preiss Book.''
''A Bantam little rooster book.''
Summary: Rhymed text and illustrations relate how
Wizard Gray changed his very gray world with color.
[1. Color—Fiction.   2. Wizards—Fiction.
3. Stories in rhyme]   I. Dillon, Leo, ill.
II. Dillon, Diane, ill.   III. Title.   IV. Series.
PZ8.3.B747Co   1989   [E]   88-7964
ISBN 0-553-05825-8
ISBN 0-553-34690-3 (pbk.)

Published simultaneously in the United States and Canada

Bantam Books are published by Bantam Books, a division of Bantam Doubleday Dell Publishing Group, Inc. Its trademark, consisting of the words
''Bantam Books'' and the portrayal of a rooster, is Registered in U.S. Patent
and Trademark Office and in other countries. Marca Registrada. Bantam
Books, 666 Fifth Avenue, New York, New York 10103.

PRINTED IN THE UNITED STATES OF AMERICA

WAK 0 9 8 7 6 5 4 3 2 1

Bank Street Ready-to-Read™

The Color Wizard

by Barbara Brenner
Illustrated by Leo and Diane Dillon

A Byron Preiss Book

A BANTAM LITTLE ROOSTER BOOK
NEW YORK · TORONTO · LONDON · SYDNEY · AUCKLAND

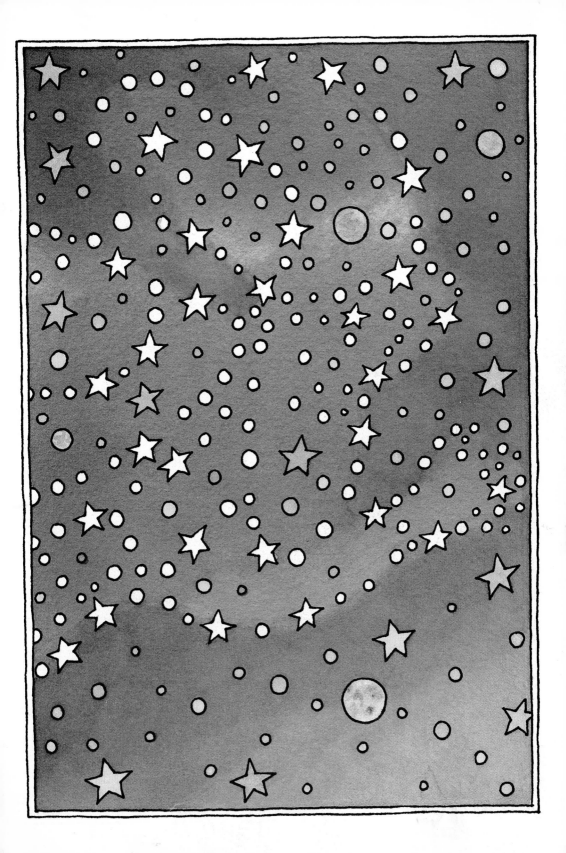

A long time ago,
and a long way away,
there lived a wizard
by the name of Gray.

He was a **brown** man.

But his beard was **gray**.
His clothes were **gray**.
From hat to shoe
that wizard was **gray**.

And that's not all.

His castle was **gray**.
His tower was **gray**.
His cats and his dragons
and his bats were **gray**.
His flowers and his grass
and his trees were **gray**.

Gray as fog.

Then one **gray** day
the wizard said,
"What we need around here
is a little **red**.

Red is bright!"

So he painted his coach.
He painted his door.
He painted his tower
from roof to floor.

His dragons said
they were wild about **red**.
So he gave each one
a dab on the head.

They looked proud!

But that color wizard
wasn't through.
"It's time," he said,
"to paint something **blue**.

Blue is cool."

So he painted his castle
and his fence all **blue**.

He painted the statues
in the garden, too.

He painted his walls.
He painted his chair.
He painted a golden sun
up in the air!

He painted the flowers.
He painted a tree.
He painted his little cats—
one, two, three.

They looked like tigers!

But then that wizard
got carried away.
He painted all night.
He painted all day!

Orange clouds. . .
tan ducks. . .

green dogs. . .
black grass. . .

purple birds. . .
white frogs.

Then he dipped his brush
into each color pail

and sailed through the sky
on a rainbow trail.

By the time that wizard
put his colors away,

there was nothing anywhere
that was **gray**.

No castles or towers
or dragons or bats,
no coaches or flowers
or statues or cats.

No **gray** on the wall.
No **gray** on the floor.
The only **gray** was the
Gray on the door.